Dedication

To Darcey Bussell

Introduction

For everyone in his class, Mr Eden was much, much more than a teacher. In fact, he was an acrobat and actor, comedian and storyteller all in one. Ryan thought he might also be a wizard in his spare time. Anya said teachers didn't have spare time, but she thought he was a sweetheart and a hero. Ryan and Anya lived on the same street. The two children weren't best friends, but their mums were like sisters. And their mums both wished they'd been in Mr Eden's class, long ago.

"He's awesome," said Anya.

"He's a legend," said Ryan.

Mr Eden was very, very funny. He knew how to make thirty children laugh loudly and happily, until their eyes were warm and wet and their stomachs felt tight. But he also knew how to make them stop laughing, the moment he wanted them to.

Mr Eden was super-fit. He could slide up and down the ropes that fell down from the

5

hall roof like a bead on an abacus. He was happy to be chased around the playground or football field, but no child ever caught him – unless he pretended to be a spider with a few missing legs. Or a jellyfish, or a Christmas pudding.

And in Dance lessons he taught Ryan, Anya and the others all kinds of different moves. He could jive. He could waltz. He could do the tango, the samba and the Charleston. But most of all, Mr Eden loved ballet.

"When we dance we tell stories," he said, "without words."

Mr Eden said that if the children listened carefully enough they could see colours in great music. He loved Story Time and sometimes he sang or hummed his own soundtrack to the books he read. At the same time he shaped his body, his face and his hands into the pictures.

"He's so funny," said Ryan. "He's insane!"

Anya laughed too, just as loudly as Ryan, but she'd noticed something else about Mr Eden. Sometimes, when the story was sad, he very nearly cried. She could see it in his eyes when she was nearly crying too. Anya liked his tears (that didn't quite fall) even more than she liked his craziness.

"He's sensitive," she told her mum. Anya liked that word because Mr Eden had used it to describe her in her report, along with 'deep'.

No one said Ryan was sensitive but he was full of what Mr Eden called 'bounce'.

For Anya and for Ryan, Story Time was the best time of the day. One afternoon, after Mr Eden had finished reading a book (one that had lit up a whole month as brightly as Christmas) the children asked what the new story was going to be.

"Aha," said Mr Eden, and made his eyes extrawide and very bright. "No book today," he added.

"Oh," groaned the children. No story! Mr Eden must be joking.

Mr Eden tapped the floppy, fair hair on the top of his head.

"I'm not going to read a story," he said. "I'm going to tell you one."

"Yay!" cried the children.

Mr Eden didn't have to ask them twice to tidy up and sit on the carpet. Ryan and Javeen had never cleaned the paint pots so quickly. Anya and Lucy had never wiped the tables so fast.

"Ready?" asked Mr Eden.

"Yes," called the children gathered on the carpet at his shiny, pointy feet.

"Steady," said Mr Eden, and wobbled like a tightrope walker over a chasm.

The children laughed. Mr Eden crossed his hands in front of his chest very quickly and the laughter stopped. He stood still for a moment, his mouth open, as if he was waiting for something in the silence, listening for it, looking out for it…

"Go!" he cried. Mr Eden was an athlete running from the starting block.

Then he remembered that he was beginning a story, not a race, and stopped still. He stood up, more like an ape than a man. He walked back to the story chair with his knuckles almost skimming the ground.

"This is a story no one has heard before, with a main character that isn't human."

Mr Eden's face didn't look quite human any more. His nostrils grew wider and his eyes stared. He looked wilder than usual.

"It's a gorilla," said Ryan.

Mr Eden became himself again and nodded. The children were enjoying the story already. Some of them made noises that were more like steam engines or crows than gorillas. Mr Eden held out a hand and they waited, silently.

"A gorilla that wanted to be," said Mr Eden, and paused, "…a ballet dancer."

He did a twirl on the spot, with his arms meeting in an arc above his head, while his face pretended to be a gorilla face and his body pretended to be heavy and hairy. Everyone laughed.

"What kind of story do you think it is?" asked Mr Eden. "Yes, Ryan? What do you think?"

"A funny one," said Ryan, grinning. "A mad one!"

Mr Eden stroked his chin and looked sideways up to the ceiling.

"It can be, yes," said Mr Eden. "This story can be total fantasy, the crazy kind. It could be about a gorilla called Gilbert and all his mates at gorilla school. If you want it to be…"

It sounded as though most of the class wanted that very much.

"But," said Mr Eden, and held one hand in the air with the fingers opening like petals from a bud to a rose. The children waited.

"It doesn't have to be," he said. "It could be the story of a gorilla called Sanyu. That's a Ugandan name and it means happiness. But this Sanyu could be sad as well as gentle."

Anya remembered seeing Mr Eden's beautiful wife. Anya's mum said Mrs Eden was from Uganda and Anya was sure she must have a pretty name.

"It could be a story full of strange, beautiful magic," said Mr Eden. "It could be about all of us."

The room was silent. For Anya, it felt as if the magic had already begun.

"What do you think, Anya?" he whispered. "Which story shall I tell? Is my gorilla Gilbert or Sanyu?"

Anya's smile was shy. "Sanyu," she said, quietly, and already she was sorry for the gorilla with sadness in his eyes.

"Ryan?" asked Mr Eden.

"Gilbert!" cried Ryan, with a gorilla grunt.

"Ah," said Mr Eden, slowly. "Perhaps there are two different stories, with two different gorillas." He paused. "What do you think Gilbert is like?"

"Goofy and cool," said Javeen, "like a cartoon gorilla."

Ryan liked that idea. He stretched up his hand because now he had an idea of his own. His arm was pointed like a rocket about to be launched. Luckily Mr Eden said his name before blast-off because it was starting to ache.

"Maybe," said Ryan, "he's the kind of gorilla that dips chips in his ice cream."

That was what Ryan had wanted to do for a while.

"Two stories," said Mr Eden, holding up the palms of his hands as if there was a live story wriggling in each one, "and I'm going to tell them both."

And he did.

Both Mr Eden's stories are here in this book.

So now you can choose.

For Sanyu, turn to page 54.
For Gilbert, read on.

GILBERT THE GORILLA

One

Mr Eden paused, because stories need silence. Palms down, he smoothed and patted the air to mark out the space for this one to grow. Someone giggled. Ryan's fists were bouncy on his thighs, and his chest thought he was on a trampoline. Mr Eden didn't frown or bark but only waited.

Then he sat up straight, let his mouth lift at the edges, and began.

Your school isn't for gorillas, although one or two sneak into the dining hall from time to time, and eat all the bananas in sight. Then they kindly leave the skins for the teachers to slide on, for your entertainment.

In this story there's a school that was rather like yours, except that the gorilla pupils grunted more often than you do, and scratched a lot. It had high green walls and the plants were taller than the teachers, but anyone who ate one – a plant, not a teacher – was put in detention.

Gilbert's friend Gaz nibbled the leaves when the teacher wasn't looking so the plants in their classroom never grew any taller. Then he looked innocently out of the window when his insides made more noise than anyone else's. When he answered a question, he hoped his teeth didn't have green bits wrapping them like braces.

Gorillas may look scary, and know how to sound scary when they need to, but they're not as fierce as they seem.

Gilbert was a very friendly gorilla who had never been known to frighten anyone. He was a cheerful, helpful gorilla, the kind to be picked. Not for bugs in his hair, although gorillas do that for each other every day. Gilbert was the sort of gorilla who was picked for responsible jobs in school and invited to birthday parties. Teachers often chose him to help the gorillas who found school hard, or partner the gorillas who forgot how to behave.

Everyone liked Gilbert, but Gaz, Gertie and Groover were his best gorilla friends.

Groover the Mover liked to pose so other gorillas could admire him. He wore sunglasses that were bigger and blacker than his gorilla eyes. For a chunky young gorilla, he had style. Groover even had rhythm, but it was the slow, heavy kind.

Because each gorilla leg weighed about the same as one Year Two child, gorillas didn't dart or flicker, swing or swoop. They left the high jump to the antelopes and the sprint to the big cats. Gorillas were less like birds and more like tree stumps.

But they made a lot more noise and had a lot more fun.

Especially Gilbert.

Gilbert was no better at swimming or climbing than other gorillas but he could do something that might surprise you. It certainly surprised Gilbert.

I don't mean dipping chips in his ice cream because Gaz gave him that idea.

I don't mean wearing a baseball cap backwards because Groover showed him how to do that without bending his ears out.

I don't mean blowing bubble gum balloons until his gorilla teeth were as pink as piglets – less muddy, but stickier.

Gilbert had a secret. Something he could do, beautifully. Something he never let anyone see. It made him both excited and calm. But he was afraid that if the other gorillas knew, they'd point their fat gorilla fingers and make fun of him.

Gilbert was the world's first and only ballet-dancing gorilla.

And it was thrilling. But it was a lonely thing to be.

None of the other gorillas knew the first thing about ballet – even if the first thing was how to spell it. Groover liked to think he could hip hop, but however hip he tried to be, he couldn't really hop, not without falling over. He was much too solid.

Gaz's favourite trick was head-butting fruit from the trees. Even though he could bounce a melon from foot to knee before he ate it, he wasn't graceful about it. In fact, it was rather a messy and grunty business.

You see, gorillas are not exactly elegant. Gertie was Scrabble champ because she knew words like

finesse but she didn't actually *have* any herself. Most gorillas would rather wrestle than dance, and Greg, who was the tallest and heaviest in Gilbert's class, did plenty of wrestling. It usually involved throwing smaller gorillas around, or holding them like baguettes under his arms.

So Gilbert was shy about ballet.

He twirled after dark.

He practised his pliés before the others were awake.

He made sure he never balanced on the tips of his toes when the other apes, the long-tailed ones, were high in the trees looking out for gossip.

But sometimes, when the teacher sent him to the stock cupboard for art straws or gold paper, he pirouetted rather carefully between the shelves before he returned to the classroom, smiling.

Gilbert was improving all the time.

He had technique.

He had poise.

He had better balance than a flamingo. He was smoother than a swan.

Soon Gilbert would be ready to show the world what he could do. And hope the world was ready.

Mr Eden had no book to close but it was time for the class to go home. He sat down instead, because he'd been standing – and dancing – through the first part of his story. As the children left, they talked about Gilbert and Groover and what would happen next. And when Mr Eden looked out through the window he saw so much scratching and grunting that for a moment he thought he was still inside his own story.

Two

The next afternoon Mr Eden began again, a few minutes early because Ryan and some of the others were having such trouble waiting.

One morning when Gilbert arrived at school he found something shiny and red parked in the playground, tucked into the shade of huge tropical leaves. It looked new and very cool. Gilbert guessed whose it was. Groover the Mover had found a new way to get around – faster.

Gilbert was admiring the bright red skateboard when Groover jumped him from behind. Gilbert kept his balance and it was Groover who wobbled briefly. Then he adjusted his sunglasses and put one big gorilla foot on the skateboard. He grinned as if someone might want a photograph.

"Want a go, dude?" he asked.

"Great!" said Gilbert, because he already knew how to balance and spin.

"It's not as easy as it looks," warned Groover. "But I can give you lessons."

"Thanks," said Gilbert.

Groover talked him through some moves but the words didn't quite match the actions that went with them. Groover sounded like an expert but he didn't really have the skateboard under control. By the time he'd been tipped off three times, his laugh was rather nervous.

Gilbert thought his hairy backside might be rather sore. Groover gave it a rub as he took a break and offered the skateboard to Gilbert.

"That might not seem... you know, super-amazing to you," said Groover, trying not to sound embarrassed, "but wait till you've seen how hard it is."

Gilbert was beginning to think skateboarding might be impossible after all.

"I know I make it look easy," said Groover, remembering how cool he was. "But beginners like you should expect to eat dirt!"

Imagining being flung off with a bump, Gilbert gave his own hairy backside a rub in advance. He positioned himself while Groover gave him more instructions.

"No," said Groover, "like this…"

But Gilbert was off. He was riding the board, swerving around the plants and trees, his thick gorilla arms outstretched.

"Gilbert!" called Groover. "Look out!"

In fact the other gorillas were looking – at

Gilbert. He was quite a sight. In and out he dodged, his balance perfect. He didn't hunch his shoulders. His head was high. And when he saw the teacher straight ahead of him, cycling to school on his rusty old bike, Gilbert did what he had to do. He angled the red board round a corner and jumped – landing back on the shiny red surface. Perfectly.

"Impressive, Gilb..." said the teacher, turning to look and falling off his bike.

Some of the young gorillas laughed at the teacher with his legs in the air, but most of them clapped Gilbert. Some of them made the kind of noises gorillas used to show admiration.

Gilbert was having fun. He knew how to have even more. Recklessly, he stood on his toes and did a quick pirouette on the board, landing gracefully. No bottom rubs needed.

"Whoah!" called Gertie. "Unorthodox!" she added, which would have scored her a lot of points in Scrabble. Gilbert couldn't tell whether unorthodox was a good thing.

"What kind of move was THAT?" asked Gaz.

"What are you doing?" cried Groover, charging over. He didn't sound as cool as usual. "Give it back before you wreck it."

Groover tucked it under his arm and headed back to the playground – without waiting for Gilbert and without turning round.

"Crazy!" said Gaz, slapping one hand to his head. It would have been two but the other held a banana he'd dipped in moss.

Gilbert thought Groover made a comment too, but he muttered it at the ground as he walked ahead. Gilbert thought he heard, "Looked like a girl to me." But a gust of wind fluttered a large leaf and he couldn't be sure.

For the rest of the day Groover seemed busy with other friends, and behind his sunglasses his mood wasn't easy to read. Gilbert didn't worry. He wasn't the kind of gorilla to fret over what *might* be and what *could* happen. Or what Groover probably didn't say.

He noticed after school that Groover and the red skateboard disappeared rather quickly, leaving a track of flattened grass in their wake. If Groover fell off during the ride home he bit his gorilla lips and kept his groans in his chest. Gilbert heard nothing but the wind and the clack of the birds in the trees. But as he listened he could picture Groover silently rubbing his backside, his face extra-dark and his mouth pulled tight.

That night, Gilbert did his ballet practice later than usual, wrapped in a thicker cloak of darkness to keep him safe. Remembering his pirouette on the skateboard helped him to spin faster and reach higher.

But remembering Groover made him wobble ever so slightly on his toes.

Gilbert grunted and hit himself on the nose with one fist – which meant, *keep dancing*. But he packed a little too much power with his punch. For a while his wide gorilla nostrils lay squashed on his face like the grass under Groover's bottom.

He felt dizzier than usual when he sneaked in by the back door – and found his mother with her hands on her gorilla hips.

"Gilbert?" she asked, holding the iron over the board like a telephone. "Where have you been? What are you up to?"

Gilbert stood, still a little dazed, in the doorway. He felt as if his nose was steaming like the iron.

"Exercising, Mum," said Gilbert slowly, because he didn't lie. He reached out one arm. "Let me do that for you. One last exercise."

Gilbert took the iron and smoothed his dad's spotty underpants, which were rather enormous

and would make Groover laugh out loud. Just like Gilbert's rather enormous dad would laugh out loud, if he knew his gorilla son was a ballet dancer.

Once his mum had kissed his sore nose and sung her way to the kitchen, Gilbert breathed out a long puff of air, rather like the iron.

His secret didn't seem as safe as it used to. And it felt a lot heavier than the iron.

Mr Eden's hands never looked heavy, and as he'd told the story they had been up in the air and down below his waist. They'd been curled and spiky and fast and slow, but now they closed, palm to palm.

The children knew it was time to go home. Some of them were quite tired from laughing. There was quite a lot of bottom rubbing on the way out, a few boys punched their noses and Ryan pretended he was skateboarding through the door – which wasn't easy.

Someone announced that there were twenty-three hours and forty-eight minutes until the next part of the story.

Three

The next day at 3:00 Ryan said he wanted to hear more about Groover. Someone muttered that Gilbert was a wuss but Mr Eden didn't seem to hear. Even though she'd wanted another kind of story, Anya made it to the front row first, looking up when Mr Eden began.

Gilbert's life remained quite normal for a while. There were chips to dip into ice cream and bananas to swallow whole. There were bugs to pick from his friends' hairy chests and birds to out-shout when they made a flappy fuss. There were jokes to laugh at and footballs to kick at playtime. Gilbert's ballet training was making him faster and stronger, and harder to tackle.

"Elegant play, Gilbert," said his P.E. teacher, after he'd swerved round two players, kept control of the ball and almost scored.

The other gorillas didn't aim for elegance. They were better at shoving. Gorillas sometimes missed the ball and toppled into the net head first. Gorillas sometimes piled up on the pitch like old coats at a jumble sale.

"Elegant play, Gilbert," teased Groover in a high voice.

He tried to wiggle, but gorillas weren't very good at wiggling either. Groover stumbled and wasn't very pleased when Gaz laughed.

But the real trouble came a few days later. It arrived with the motorbike.

Gilbert heard it before he saw it, and at first he thought it was a new gorilla noise, from a fierce, deep throat. Or a hairy stomach.

The lush grass quivered. Then it flattened weakly on both sides of the fat wheels as they rolled, faster than logs. The trees shook water droplets through the sunlight, and they made the paintwork gleam. Towards the playground the motorbike roared, like a lion on the rampage.

Astride it was something hairy, with a short leather jacket flapping open like wings. The rider was pressing in with chunky legs and leaning over the handlebars with gorilla grip. Even though he wore a large, shiny helmet, Gilbert guessed whose head was inside it. He thought he could see sunglasses through the visor.

The air was hotter than usual, with a sharp new taste.

Gaz, Gertie and the other gorillas lumbered over excitedly and some of them couldn't help hooting as Groover swung himself slowly from the saddle.

Groover the Mover leaned the bike against a tree and lifted off his helmet, which made his sunglasses fly off and land like a dead bird with two legs in the air. Gaz tried not to laugh as Gertie picked them up for him. Groover swung his shoulders as if losing his sunglasses was part of his show. He placed them above his gorilla nostrils, smiled and bowed. He looked back at the motorbike with love, as if he'd like to pat it.

"Cool, Groover!" called Gaz.

Groover lifted his gorilla thumbs. "Always have been," he said.

"I meant the motorbike," muttered Gaz, but Groover didn't seem to hear.

"Can you do a wheelie?" asked someone.

"What tricks can you do, Groover?" asked someone else.

Groover ignored the questions. Maybe the engine had made him deafer than usual. Lots of gorillas wanted a ride on the motorbike but Gilbert didn't ask, because he had the feeling he knew what the answer would be – and it would begin with 'n' and end in 'o'.

But Gilbert had seen a picture in his imagination and it wouldn't go away. He had to test it, and see if it could be real.

It was a while before he had the chance.

After school it was rugby training. Whenever Gilbert had the ball, he found himself tackled – from behind, from below, from right and left, and always by the same gorilla. Four times Groover upended him. Four times Gilbert had his breath snatched from him. Four times he lost the world in a cloud of dust that also coated his teeth.

"Take a break, Gilbert," said the teacher.

So he sat and watched. It was only a few minutes before Groover scored a try. The rest of the team mobbed him and the spectators cheered. Gilbert clapped and smiled as Groover ran around the pitch and beat his gorilla chest.

At half-time Gilbert wandered off for a stroll, and when he reached the motor bike he wondered what would happen if he started up the engine.

He only meant to find out whether he could ride it – not like a biker but a dancer. As the engine revved into life it reminded him of a lion poked with a branch and ready to bite. Calmly, because this was only a machine with no teeth and no claws, Gilbert balanced on the seat and pointed one leg backwards in an arabesque. One arm held the handlebars and the other curved above his head.

The motorbike underneath him was speeding off. Like an admiring crowd, the trees on all sides waved their leaves as he whizzed past them. Gilbert felt the air tug his hair and scour his face but he didn't wobble. Every time he almost hit a rock, a snake, a tree trunk or a lizard, he swerved at the last minute and sped past or round it.

But with his eyes down, Gilbert didn't see that he was heading towards the school field. He didn't see the players stop and stare. Gilbert had let go of the handlebars and was spinning on the seat, twirling as he raced. All he saw were the gorilla legs running or diving out of the way. The engine drowned their grunts and hoots and he was moving much too quickly to see the alarm on their faces.

He did see the H-shaped goal post ahead of him – but only just, and his hands were lifted too high in the air to grab the handlebars in time. As the front wheel hit the post, Gilbert flew up, leaving the bike to fall away behind him. Arms stretched, legs spread, toes pointed, he was soaring as high as a goal kick. In fact, he *was* a goal kick. Like a ball with a boot behind it he was rising and spinning...

until his nose, which was upward, tilted down again. He hurtled, head first, towards the ground.

Gilbert's nostrils were clogged with dust and mud – and a beetle that struggled out with the help of one finger. As he pulled his nose back into shape it started to sting again. His ears felt hot and tight, as if they'd been stretched until they pinged.

Slowly Gilbert felt the world settle around him. For a moment it seemed oddly quiet. Then he realised that Groover was observing him. Hard. He was sitting on the motorbike, which was silent and still like a wild horse that had been tamed. With no scratches or dents, it was shiny as ever. But Groover's arms were folded across a puffed-up chest, and his nostrils were wide. Gilbert couldn't see through his sunglasses but he didn't think Groover was happy.

Gilbert was coated in mud. It stiffened like chocolate setting hard around a filling. But it didn't taste the same when some of it slipped into his mouth. Gilbert stretched. The mud cracked and fell off in pieces, like egg shell when you tap it in the egg cup.

The other gorillas were open-mouthed, but not for long. Laughter was starting to fill the silence and it was just as loud as the engine could be, and just as spluttery. Especially Gaz's, because he was eating melon at the time and the pips sprayed like rain. Several gorilla heads got decorated and the melon juice meant they stuck.

At first Gilbert didn't mind. They were an audience and they were having fun. But then he heard something in the laughter that stopped him feeling the same kind of happiness. It was a sound that rubbed his nose in the mud all over again. It was a sound that squashed him.

He heard a few words amongst the hoots and grunts. *Own goal specialist. Eating dirt again.*

Someone flapped wings and tried to squawk because he'd flown. Someone asked whether he'd *got a kick out of that*. Gertie called him the world's only *aerodynamic* gorilla and Groover laughed as if that made him a freak.

Gilbert started to feel that this audience wouldn't be the kind to clap at the end. They'd be the kind to throw banana skins.

If anyone had noticed the perfect line of his arabesque, no one was impressed. He'd made a hairy great fool of himself. He hurried off, stiffer than usual, to get a shower.

Now Gilbert knew for sure that if he were to dance for them, really dance, this was the sound he'd hear. They'd think he was every bit as ridiculous as a gorilla hurled over a goal post and nose-diving into mud.

Gilbert told himself to stop dreaming.

Now.

Mr Eden told the class that he was afraid they must stop dreaming too. Ryan decided to ask his mum for at least one banana for lunch the next day. On the playground he gave Mr Eden a double thumbs-up through the window, and Mr Eden smiled.

Four

At Story Time next day Mr Eden said he knew how much children liked a laugh, and teachers did too. So did gorillas.

The children in his class were smiling even before he continued the story.

For the rest of that week, the jokes continued.

"There goes Gilbert," the gorillas said, when a plane flew overhead.

"Is that Gilbert?" asked a giggly Gertie when a bird cawed above the trees.

"No, *that's* Gilbert!" said Groover, pointing to a plop that landed on the forest floor as another bird took off and left it behind.

Gilbert was clean now, and his bruises were fading. But the jokes kept on coming.

"Ho ho," he said, and made sure he smiled.

Gilbert didn't feel much like practising his ballet steps any more, but *not* dancing felt wrong. It made him ache on the inside. So he kept up his training, but more secretly than ever, sneaking out by dusk like a gorilla burglar.

Then Monday came round and packed a surprise.

It began as a sound: a happy tune that wound its way through the trees like a shiny birthday ribbon. A ribbon of song. But it was a while before Gilbert saw the singer.

It was Groover who brought the surprise with him, at quarter to nine on Monday morning, carrying a lunchbox and a book bag, both clearly named. *Gladys.* She was half his height and half his weight. Gladys was starting in Reception and she sounded very excited. She was skipping along beside Groover, with a fat velvet ribbon tied in a bow on top of her head, and she was still singing.

"Morning, Groover," said Gilbert.

"Where's your motorbike?" asked Gaz.

"My sister is way noisier than a motorbike," groaned Groover. "It's her birthday and she won't stop."

Gladys started skipping. Holding her hand, Groover found himself jolted about and scuttling to keep up with her. He couldn't stop her singing even though he covered his ears as if he wished he could.

But Gilbert liked the sound that burst and flowed from Gladys. The tune had no words but it didn't only bounce. It swelled like a river in a flood. It splashed like a summer shower. It traced the silence lightly like a breeze… and surged back like a storm lashing rocks – only to bubble back again and sparkle as if the sun had broken through.

Gilbert stood, grinning from one gorilla ear to another. It was music to dance to. What Gladys sang was a story and it made him want to pirouette across the playground and leap through his classroom door.

"She never shuts up," said Groover. "It does my head in."

But he smiled, because Gladys sang better than the birds. She looked funny too, with her ribbon squeezing a few gorilla hairs into a spiky bunch in the middle of her head. There was a gap between her two front teeth and her skipping style was lumpy and bumpy.

Gilbert winked at Gladys.

Gladys tried to wink back at Gilbert. But all she managed to do was tilt her head to one side and squeeze both eyes tight, into little slits. Then they burst open again, wider and brighter than before. And all the time she kept on singing.

"What an embarrassment," said Groover, as she paused her song just long enough to place a kiss on his cheek. Of course she couldn't reach all around Groover to hug him but she tried.

"Bye, Glad!" said Groover. "Gerroff!"

Groover gave Gladys a quick pat on the head and left her to line up outside the Reception door as the bell rang. When it stopped, Gladys was still singing, as quietly as a stream.

"Glad to escape," Groover told his friends, with a grimace that was also a grin.

"She's somewhat unconventional," said Gertie.

"Your sister's nuts," said Gaz, laughing, and pulled a fluffy old cashew out of his trouser pocket.

"Yeah," said Groover. "She's got music where her brains should be!"

Gilbert could still hear the music. It filled his head as he put his things in his drawer and sat down for the register.

On the outside, Gilbert was reading, writing, adding and taking away, but on the inside he was dancing, all through the day.

He saw Gladys at playtime, skipping and singing. Gilbert winked. Gladys covered one eye with a gorilla hand and grinned, but she didn't stop singing. Even when she was playing a game with some of her new classmates, Gilbert could still hear the song, volume low, like a soundtrack to a film.

"Has she always been full of music?" he asked.

"No," said Groover. "When she was a baby she was full of wind." He laughed and the others laughed too. "The music only started a week or two ago. Mum asked her where it came from and she said it's a secret. But I'll make her tell."

Gilbert didn't think anything of Gladys's secret, not at first.

But that evening, when all good gorillas were tucked up in bed, Gilbert began to practise his ballet steps. Holding on to a branch that was just the right height, he bent his legs and balanced on one at a time, warming up his muscles. In his head he heard some music, just like the song without words Gladys had sung at school. It sounded so real that he began to hum as he danced, letting the music lead him.

As Gilbert pirouetted, the tune spun around his twirling body like candyfloss wrapping around the stick. He landed with both arms raised, and listened, because he wasn't sure any more that the music was inside his head. Gilbert could hear the birds and the breeze. He could hear the soft snap of twigs breaking under feet. But there was something more. The trees were singing, and the music belonged to his dance.

For a crazy moment Gilbert pictured trees holding violins across their trunks and bows in their branches. But then he heard a sound that made him catch his breath. Something bounced. It stopped, but the song went on. Gilbert tiptoed towards it, and when it ended, all of a sudden, he kept on advancing towards the forest.

Something short, chunky and hairy was covering its mouth and eyes as if it wanted to disappear. Its gorilla shoulders were hunched and its gorilla knees were bent but it couldn't hide. Gilbert recognised the red ribbon – rather grubby now – that hung off the end of its short hairy topknot.

"Glad," said Gilbert.

Gladys opened her eyes and uncovered her mouth. "Oh-oh!" she said.

"Am I your secret?" asked Gilbert.

"Yes," she said, "I've been watching you. You're the best secret ever!"

She tried a pirouette but stumbled and fell into Gilbert. She held her head as if it might spin off, or drop like a coconut. Gilbert steadied her.

"I can't dance," she said.

"But you can sing, Gladys," Gilbert told her.

"You can dance, Gilbert," she said, excitedly, clapping her gorilla hands. "You gave me the music. Your dancing put it in my head."

Gilbert smiled. "Really?"

Gladys bounced three times. Gilbert thought that was probably a *yes*.

"I'm glad, Glad," he said, "that you've been my secret audience. Would you be my secret orchestra too?"

Gladys bounced until she fell into a tree and bumped her nose but she didn't seem to care. Gilbert sprang back to the middle of the clearing and waited, head down, knees bent. His arms hung low and met like a cradle for a gorilla baby.

Gladys began. Out of her gorilla throat came the music that matched the dance. Gladys sang. Gilbert danced, and his dancing made Gladys so happy that she sang better than ever.

He leapt higher and further. He leapt over logs, and snakes that were too surprised to attack. Then he leapt over Gladys when she sat down for a rest.

He spun faster – not just on the spot and in a whole string of spins that crossed the clearing, but around Gladys. Then, picking her up and holding her like a picture he wanted to show the class, he spun with her in his arms. He spun so fast that her red bow spun too, right off her hairy gorilla head. The birthday ribbon flew off through the trees and wrapped a branch like a present.

His gorilla body stretched tighter and taller than ever before. It bent lower and smaller. Gilbert's sharp shapes were sharp enough to cut the air and his soft shapes were so light they almost floated away.

The happy moves felt like goals. The sad moves were so heartbreaking he was relieved to feel his own gorilla heart, still beating – fast but strong. His legs had the spring of a gazelle and at times his arms seemed to think they were wings.

So by the time Gilbert had finished – just as Gladys's song held its last, clear note – he was very tired but very happy too.

Gilbert managed to murmur a *thank you* as he bowed. That was before he fell to the ground with his gorilla arms and legs spread out, and his gorilla chest rising and falling like the waltz.

"You were amazing," said Gladys. "You gave me my best song."

It was time for bed but Gilbert managed one more word as he sprang up, collected his breath and tried to keep it under control.

"Secret?" he asked.

"Top top top C-cret!" sang Gladys, with a note higher than the tree tops.

Gilbert let her ride him home.

At the word *home* the children understood. Some of them groaned. In the corridor Anya tried a very secret high note but it was better inside her head. Then she rolled her eyes because outside on the playground Ryan was catching a ride on Charlie's back, crying, "Take me home!"

Five

The following day the class gathered in silence on the carpet. The speed was record-breaking. Mr Eden began straight away.

Now Gilbert wasn't alone any more. It felt good to be part of a team. Or at least, a duo. Just thinking of Gladys made Gilbert chuckle. It made his toes point and his fingers stretch.

They danced together every night, and every day at school they winked across the playground. At least, Gilbert winked. Gladys twitched, or blinked both eyes shut, or covered one as if it was a game of peep-o.

Then one day, when the bell rang for the school day to begin, there was no Groover and no Gladys either.

"Maybe they're sick," said Gaz. "Tummy bug."

Gaz often had a funny tummy because of the things he mixed inside his: jelly and cheese, bulbs and custard, or termites and jam.

"Maybe they overslept," said Gertie, and laughed at the very idea.

Gilbert laughed too, because as he pointed out, "Gladys is part-gorilla and part-alarm clock."

"And Groover doesn't know how to switch her off," said Gertie.

But by the time the teacher had taken the register there was still no sign of Groover.

"Gilbert," said Mr Grunt, "Take this note to Reception, please."

He knocked on the Reception door and waited to be told to enter. As he walked in and saw all the little gorillas cross-legged on the carpet, he knew straight away that Gladys wasn't one of them. No song. Not even a whisper of music, and no bouncing either.

When she read the note Miss Hoot said, "Oh dear. I hope there's no emergency."

Gilbert didn't like the sound of that word. He pictured nasty germs swirling like midges around Gladys and Groover. He imagined the germs opening fierce little mouths and biting their skin – and taking Gladys's song away.

Maybe she'd never get it back again.

But perhaps it was a different emergency. Maybe Gladys was locked in the bathroom. She might be singing in the bath while Groover and his mum and dad tried to batter down the door. If the water cooled she'd catch a cold that would go to her chest – and take her song away.

Gilbert was panicking. What if Gladys was lost and the rest of the family were searching for her? What if she was stuck in mud and couldn't tug herself free? What if a crocodile had bitten off her head?

Gilbert's gorilla mouth started to wobble and he had to push away one gorilla tear with his fist. Then he remembered that he wasn't the sort of gorilla to panic. Imagination was there to be used, and Gilbert planned to make very good use of his.

Gilbert had a reply to deliver to Mr Grunt but he didn't take it himself. He posted Miss Hoot's note under his classroom door for Mr Grunt to find. Then he headed for the gym, climbed the rope and swung it out of the open window. Landing on the school field, Gilbert jumped up and ran towards the forest.

He tried the house where Groover and Gladys lived. Their dad's sports car was parked outside but it was empty and there was no one at home.

"Groover!" he called, running on. "Gladys!"

There was no answer but he kept running. Gilbert leapt over one log in an *assemblé*, jumping from one foot and landing on two. All his ballet training had made him fast and fit. Over the next log he tried an *entrechat*, crossing his legs in the air. As he ran, he listened. No song. But no screaming either. No alarm barks. Just birds making a fuss as usual, flip-flapping about, backwards and forwards, gossiping.

"Where's Gladys?" he asked them, but they answered at once and all Gilbert heard was a clash of squawks like out-of-tune violins.

"Show me!" he cried, but they didn't understand gorilla grunts any more than he understood bird call.

The sun was fierce and Gilbert's head was hot on the inside too. He knew he must keep going. Now he reached the river. There might be crocs under the water, ready to surface and snatch with open jaws. Gorillas couldn't swim, but Gilbert could jump. It would be quicker than taking the long way round, over the bridge. But could he make it all the way across in one leap? Because Gilbert knew that if his jump didn't measure up, he'd land with one tasty leg in the river for a crocodile to snack on!

From one side to the other Gilbert leapt, skimming the tips of the grass that sprouted tall at the water's edge. In a huge *grand jeté* he stretched his legs wide in the air, like scissors pulled open as far as they'll go without snapping. Gilbert didn't snap. But a crocodile tried. It lifted a suspicious head and opened its greedy jaws. Luckily for Gilbert, he was much too fast and much too high. The croc was much too late. All it saw was a hairy blur ahead of its snout as Gilbert rejoined dry land and raced away again.

But a few strides later, Gilbert stopped. He listened carefully, because ahead of him he could

hear voices, one after another and sometimes overlapping.

"Come down, Gladys!"

"You can do it!"

"Just JUMP, will you!"

Gilbert charged on, looking up into the branches of the tallest tree in the forest.

"Eeeeee!" cried Gladys, in a high and wobbly protest from above. It was almost a note, cut off from a tune.

Gilbert saw her, a long way up the tree, clutching the trunk as if it was her mummy. But her real mummy was below, looking anxious. Her daddy looked weary, and Groover huffed as if he had no patience left. Gorillas could climb, but Gladys was well over the limit.

"What are you doing up there, Glad?" asked Gilbert.

"I thought I'd make my high C even higher," said Gladys, feebly.

Groover put one gorilla hand to his forehead and sighed.

"Maybe now you'll stop singing," he huffed.

"Oh, no!" said Gilbert.

The other three stared at him.

"Why not?" they asked, all at once. "Gorillas don't sing."

"Gladys does," said Gilbert, "beautifully."

Up in the tree Gladys managed a very weak smile.

"Singing's no use to gorillas," said her dad.

Gilbert didn't say it was useful to him, and magical too. He didn't waste any more time. Instead he looked up at Gladys and gave her a wink.

"Trust me, Glad," he said, and stood on his gorilla toes, reaching up his gorilla arms in a perfect open arch that reached towards Gladys.

Gladys smiled. Holding on to Gilbert's hands she stepped onto his shoulders. Gilbert swung her

down and round so that her head pointed towards the grass in a fish dive. Her arms hung loose but her feet were on both sides of his gorilla neck. Gladys wasn't scared. She trusted Gilbert completely, even when she might have opened her mouth and grazed on the grass as she hung upside down. He spun her round and turned her the right way up, safe and steady. As she landed, she opened her mouth in a smile that was wide enough to let out a new song.

Gilbert spun as the music thickened and lifted. There was no stopping him now. He was dancing with delight, because no one had taken Gladys's music away. And Gladys had never sung so freely. The music burst out of the forest, carried by the wind, out towards the school.

There in the ICT suite, Gilbert's classmates were working on the computers. Through the low buzz of warm technology trickled the song of an excited gorilla. Twenty-eight gorilla heads lifted and looked to the windows.

Mr Grunt's gorilla face creased with curiosity.

"That's Gladys," said Gaz, once he'd taken his pencil tip out of his mouth. Before that, it sounded like *ra-radish*.

"I didn't know," said Mr Grunt, "that she could sing so beautifully."

"Please, sir," said Gertie, "may we investigate?"

Mr Grunt thought beautiful music should not be ignored. He led the class in an orderly line through the forest towards it. The gorillas were all very sensible because they didn't want to miss a note of the song. Even Gaz was too busy listening to chew anything on the way. Over the bridge they marched, as lightly as ants – well, nearly – so that they didn't disturb the music. As they walked on, it grew louder and finer.

Suddenly Mr Grunt lifted a gorilla finger.

Through a gap in the trees something was moving. Whatever it was, it seemed to be right at the centre of the song. But it moved so fast, it was hard to tell what it could be or what it was doing, on the ground one minute and in the air the next.

"Groover!" mouthed Gaz.

All they saw was Groover's back, in his little leather jacket. Groover didn't see them, because his eyes were on the movement too: the dark, hairy, fast, leaping, twirling, bending, bouncing, stretching movement that twisted and flowed between the trees and reached up to their branches.

Groover's parents kept their eyes on the same spilling splash of furry movement. They didn't even turn as Mr Grunt and all the gorilla pupils joined them without a word. Together the audience made a semi-circle, like the front row of the Stalls in a theatre. Together they made a hush. Like owls their eyes were round. Like bubble-blowing fish they had mouths that opened wide. The movement was Gilbert dancing.

The audience had grown now but Gilbert hardly noticed. His turning, tilting world was still only to spin again. He made circles and angles and lines. He had bounce and flight and grace and stamina. Gilbert was dancing as no gorilla had ever danced before.

But no dance is for ever. As the final note held him still, Gilbert heard his heart, full in his chest. He felt his hot, fast breaths. With a last surge of will, he lifted Gladys across his shoulders and turned, round and round, until her legs were spinning like the spokes of a wheel around his head. For a few moments Gilbert's world was a furry blur spiked with grass and framed with leaves. Then he stopped. In the silence he held Gladys high, her arms raised towards the sun.

Now, for the first time, Gilbert saw the faces staring.

Gaz looked as if he'd sat on something very hot – or eaten something even hotter!

Gertie looked as if she'd had a dream that might be a nightmare.

Groover looked as if his leather jacket was made of iron. The grown-up gorillas held their heads as if they throbbed…

But not for long.

"Bravo!" cried Groover's dad.

"Extraordinary!" cried Mr Grunt, and when he began to clap all the other gorillas clapped too.

"A-ma-zing!" cried Groover, and when he stamped his feet all Gilbert's classmates stamped theirs too.

The ground shook. The termites trembled and the ants were anxious, but the gorillas were far too busy to eat them. In fact they were too busy cheering and whooping to do anything except clap and stomp and cry out:

"Woweee!"

"Fab-u-lous!"

"Yeahhhhhhhhhhhhhhhhhhhhhhhhhhhhhh!"

"Hoorah!"

"Yayyyyyyyyyyyyyyyyyyyyyyyy!"

and the occasional "Ow!" when someone stamped on someone else's foot.

Gilbert didn't say a word. He lowered Gladys safely to the ground, where she made a wobbly kind of curtsey. He just bowed very stylishly, and smiled rather shyly. He was still bowing when a bunch of flowers landed at his feet.

Gilbert looked up to find his mum. She must have lost one floppy slipper and one dangly earring when she rushed towards the music.

"Go on, then, darling," she said, and blew her nose. "You must be hungry after that!"

Gilbert grinned and took a juicy bite of the fullest bloom. He enjoyed every drop of nectar, each soft petal and chewy stem – even though Gaz said any bouquet would be tastier with ketchup and custard. When Gilbert swallowed the last leaf, the crowd even clapped his burp.

Gilbert felt almost perfectly happy, except that when he looked around the audience, his father wasn't there. He'd missed the show.

Still Gilbert's fans clapped and stamped their feet. Groover was so inspired he did some disco moves, tripped on a tree root and landed in an accidental handstand. Everyone laughed, including Groover – even when a monkey ran off with his sunglasses.

From the back of the crowd Gilbert heard a roar: "More, more! Encore!" He looked for Gladys to lift one last time, but she was chasing the monkey and trying to grab its tail. So he did a crowd-pleasing action replay of his longest, highest leap and fastest pirouette. It left him breathless.

As he bowed again, he lost the ground under his tired feet.

"My son!" he heard, as he found himself on giant silverback shoulders.

Holding him high, Gilbert's proud father began a final round of cheers. Then he led the way home.

Like a Cup-winning team, the gorillas paraded back through the forest – with Gilbert as their captain, their goal scorer and their trophy.

Mr Eden looked as if he was holding his own son high on his shoulders. He was smiling, and when he looked down on the faces of the children in his class, he saw that they were smiling too.

"And the head teacher closed the school," he added, "to celebrate."

"Go, Gilbert!" cried Ryan.

"Home time," said Mr Eden.

"But there'll be another story tomorrow, won't there?" asked Anya.

"Oh yes," said Mr Eden. "Every day needs a story. A day without a story is a day without light."

Outside, the winter darkness was starting to fall, but Anya could imagine the sun's warmth on gorilla hair.

She smiled, because stories were worth waiting for.

SANYU

1

The children were ready for a different kind of story. In the classroom at three o'clock they felt the change all around them.

Anya watched as Mr Eden smoothed the story space. His hands might have been stroking the surface of the stillest water. His eyes were not laughing now, but wondering. He began to look around the classroom as if he didn't recognise it, and it astonished him. As he gazed upward, the children's eyes lifted too.

Mr Eden leaned forward just a little, his eyes on the ceiling, one hand spread open to touch the silence.

Then he began.

Have you seen the kind of forest where the trees knit a roof? Sanyu the gorilla had a roof like that, high above his world.

Have you cooled yourself in their shadows, dark and green as broccoli? Sanyu the gorilla loved to laze in those shadows.

Have you listened to the birds that thicken the air until it's stiff with music? Sanyu did, till the music gave him dreams.

For a gorilla, he lived a regular sort of life. Every day he smiled at the sun glinting through the forest roof. Sometimes he climbed just a little – as high as gorillas can – to try to pick it, like fruit from a tree. When he was hot or tired, he would lie down on the forest floor and let the shadows splash him as if they were made of water.

Sanyu was healthy, fit and strong. He could beat his gorilla chest like a drum, and knuckle-walk so fast that it was almost running. When he wasn't swinging and playing, he would scratch himself contentedly, or eat the bugs he found in his friends' hair.

Sanyu could tuck in his lips so neatly that it looked as if someone had stitched them down with a needle and thread. Like all gorillas, he could throw, slap and lunge. He had a hundred gorilla faces to show how he felt. He could grunt or hoot, whine or chuckle. He could growl or roar, and make all kinds of other sounds that humans wouldn't know how to name.

Whenever he felt inclined, he could rise up onto two legs instead of four, and see the world from a higher place. And every evening, as the light faded, Sanyu made his own bowl-shaped nest out of leaves and branches. He had a favourite, special dream.

His name meant happiness, but there was just one thing missing in his gorilla life.

Sanyu wanted to dance.

Of course Sanyu had never seen or heard of ballet, but in his dreams he stood high on his gorilla toes and spun. He leapt like a gazelle and landed like a leaf. He lifted his powerful arms and stroked the air as if it was silk. But only in his dreams, and he kept them secret. He was afraid the other gorillas might not understand.

Sanyu wanted to fit in among the blackbacks. One day he hoped to be the silverback the rest admired, the wise leader who made the big decisions. He would be proud to look after the troop and keep the youngsters safe. But for now, he was a youngster himself, along with Dembe and Kizza. There were three mothers, but only one silverback and he was in charge. His name was Mukasa and he didn't groom anyone. What an idea! The others groomed Mukasa.

Mukasa liked to be cleaned and tidied by Sanyu because of his light touch. It meant he could grasp anything he fancied with his hands and his feet: a juicy flower, a tasty treat of bark from a forest tree, or the smallest, wriggliest ant.

Sanyu held on just as tightly to his ballet dancing dream, but he didn't tell anyone.

Until he met Akello.

The girl called Akello was twelve. She lived in a village full of people but sometimes she didn't think she belonged. Akello wished she lived in a different world, where she could be herself.

Akello had rhythm. When the drums beat inside her she could shake like a maraca and bounce like a ball. But once, on a TV run by battery, she'd heard a different kind of music. It came from another time and place. The music told a story she could only dream. Akello stared at the dancers balancing like flamingos on long beautiful legs. She stared at their short, puffed-out dresses, shimmering under stage lights. Ballet! That was the kind of dancer Akello wanted to be.

If only she had a partner!

But Akello was taller than the boys. She felt less like a delicate flower drifting in breeze, and more like a tree. Little children tried to climb her. Up on her shoulders they felt brave and safe. But no one could lift Akello. Her mother thought she was a very useful daughter because she could carry huge baskets of melons. Her father was proud that she could bring home enough wood for a fire. But sometimes Akello felt sad to think that she would never be a swan, a princess or a Sugarplum Fairy.

So she made sure no one saw her pirouette. No

one knew she could stand on her toes and reach a long, slow arm to the sky. No one saw when she leapt across the stream with her head high and her legs as straight as spears.

Until she met Sanyu.

There was something about the way Mr Eden said the sentence that told everyone – even the children who couldn't tell the time from the big classroom clock – the first part of the story was over. Anya's shoulders fell and the air pushed out of her mouth with disappointment.

Anya liked Akello and she wanted her to be happy.

2

At the end of the next day, Mr Eden was very calm as the children gathered, more quietly than usual. He waited before he began.

In Uganda the day was a gentle one. It didn't bake and break the ground into cracks, or batter it with rain. The breeze was like a mother's fingertips on a hot forehead. Rising sleepily in the sky, the sun took life easy. It hadn't rained for days, or was it weeks?

Akello felt like a flower that wanted to open wide. It was a day for dancing. The blue of the sky was so soft and clear that it made a perfect stage. Her arms lifted in curves as graceful as rainbows and her toes straightened into points that raised her up, taller than ever.

Dancing was a secret that felt too big to keep. It burst out of her as she spun and leapt across the clearing at the foot of the mountain. Akello felt brave and strong. She felt alive.

For the first time, Akello didn't care whether anyone saw. But no one did. No one, that is, except a young gorilla tasting the air and letting it swell his black chest.

Sanyu thought it would be a shame to break the peace by grunting, shouting or beating that chest. Awake before the other blackbacks, he was only exercising. He knew that dancers must be fast and fit as lions. He knew his lungs must be full of freshness. Sanyu was breathing and stretching, exploring and watching the quietness, when he saw Akello.

He didn't hear her. Akello was much too light for that. But he saw her burst across the green world, stirring it into life. Her red dress twisted and swayed, like a flag tearing from a pole and flying. Even the grass seemed to murmur and clap.

As Akello landed her last leap, she stretched out her arms like branches soft with leaves. Sanyu opened his mouth and out came his surprise and delight. Out came his deep respect. He admired Akello, and envied her too, because she danced so bravely. To Sanyu she was small as a bush, but bold and beautiful as a leopard. Out came a gorilla noise that meant 'Bravo'.

The noise held Akello still. Her arms had lost their grace. Her feet clung heavily to the earth. Only her eyes moved now, as she searched the forest that edged the clearing.

Between two trees, something huge and black jumped from one foot to another. Wide dark eyes were fixed on her. Leathery skin opened up on teeth that chattered without words. She couldn't be sure, but she thought the mouth might be smiling.

In her own language Akello said, "Hello," lifting the word like a question.

"You're magnificent," said Sanyu, in gorilla-speak, but Akello didn't understand.

All she heard was grunting. She tried not to be afraid as he moved slowly towards her. As round as buttons and shiny as beetles in sunlight, those black eyes held her in their gaze.

Akello didn't know what to do or say, so she just stood as tall as she could. Of course Sanyu was taller. Even though Akello reminded herself that gorillas didn't eat girls, her legs were ready to run.

Sanyu's nostrils quivered curiously as he drew closer to the girl. He saw how small her fingers were, how light. He saw how pretty her eyes were, how delicate her feet, how slim her neck.

Sanyu had no more words. He reached out his hairy arms and took Akello's hands in his.

With a gasp, Akello felt herself turn, like the handle of a well that drew water from the warm ground.

Her heart lifted and swelled. The gorilla took her weight and held her firm as she balanced, her fingers resting on his great hairy shoulder. Akello was dancing again. She had never felt so brave or so free.

Sanyu's feet were firm as the roots of trees. Yet they had the ripple and flow of a river. When he lifted her high, the girl in his arms was as light as a twig picked from the earth. The red cloth petals of her dress spread out towards the sun above. Somehow he knew how to hold her. They danced like two blooms from the same plant, as if in the earth below they shared the same roots.

Step by step, turn by turn, lift by lift, the girl and the gorilla danced. Sanyu felt the strength in the girl's heart. However fast he spun her, however high or low he held her, Akello was fearless. Together they filled the light with shapes that spread like reflections and wove like shadows. Sanyu was dancing as he had never danced before and he was happier than he had ever been.

Dembe didn't see Akello dance with Sanyu. Neither did Kizza. If they had, they would have barked the gorilla alarm.

Mukasa didn't see Sanyu dance with Akello. If he had, he might have given both of them a serious silverback stare that made their legs shake and fold. But gorillas are near-sighted, so none of them saw a thing.

Only the birds made an audience. In the trees, excitement shook them into a fluttering, squawking muddle of applause. The village was waking, but no one saw enough to understand. If there were children who opened their eyes to glimpse a swirl of black and red through green, they didn't stare or wonder. They thought their dreams had not yet let them go.

Like a flower that must die, the dance began to end. Higher than ever, Akello felt the air around her circling like the ripples in a pool. Folding, she slipped like a shawl from the huge black shoulder. Every ballet had a final step and she knew it was over now. In her head the music held its note. And Akello held her breath.

When she opened her lungs, her eyes and her body, Sanyu had gone. But the world around her was a different place. Akello was a different girl.

Akello looked into the trees that led into the forest. She heard its sounds. She walked, lightly and boldly, towards the village.

There was water to fetch. There were melons to carry. At school there were numbers waiting to be added and subtracted. Words swarmed back into her head like insects, jostling, buzzing.

But Akello's life was new.

Anya found a wide smile on her face. Mr Eden was smiling too. She wanted to tell him that stories made the world new, but she thought he already knew.

From the end of the corridor, she looked back towards the classroom because she remembered the sadness that sometimes came into that world when no one expected it. In stories the sadness felt safer, and more like a dream.

But she'd sit at the back for the rest of this one, so that no one else would see if she cried.

3

Sanyu wore a secret smile all day. He sat on the ground in the daytime nest of branches and leaves, enjoying the forest. He smiled as he watched Kizza chew and dribble until his teeth were clogged with stems and his chin dripped.

He smiled as he listened to a chattering Dembe. She was showing off, with her chest puffed high as usual.

He smiled as the bugs were picked from his fur.

All day he took life easy, as he remembered.

At the end of the day, as the light thinned, Sanyu exercised out of sight. He stretched and bent. He practised his pirouettes and pliés. He balanced on his toes. He knew he must keep fit and supple because he was a dancer now. He had to be fast and strong for the girl with no fear.

Sleepy now, Sanyu arranged his thick legs and strong arms until he was comfortable. Still smiling, he closed his eyes. In his sleep he dreamed he was dancing, lifting the girl until they spun up into the clouds. The air around them was bright and blue and they were floating in it.

When he heard the birds make their morning song he swung down from the tree and went to find her. Sanyu's eyes scanned the clearing.

There was life all around him, swooping and flapping in the skies and cawing in the branches. There was life on the ground, scampering low with wriggly legs. But there was no girl in a red dress. Sanyu waited, watched and listened, but still she didn't come.

Sanyu headed back to the forest with a heavy tread. His shoulders drooped and his eyes had lost their shine.

Suddenly he straightened. Was she sick? Was she hurt, or in danger?

Did she need his help?

Or was she just a dream?

There was no smile on Sanyu's face as the others greeted him. With a question on her face and a gentle grunt, his mother wondered what was wrong.

Even Mukasa the silverback narrowed the eyes in his dark, strong head. But he made no sound.

Sanyu was not all right. He was afraid he would never dance again.

Mr Eden had stopped, as if school was over and the children had gone. But Anya knew the story wasn't over yet. Suddenly he saw their faces and smiled. He held up his forefinger and began again.

Akello's mother lay on her bed. Her head was hot with fever. It was hotter than the air that clung damply to her hair and dress. Restlessly, she tried to shake off the heat as she turned from one side to another. Beside her lay a baby boy, his eyes closed but his mouth open wide. Akello's father picked him up, but he kept on crying.

Akello's mother reached for him, and for a while he sucked quietly. But Akello could see how weak her mother was. She was too tired to speak and too tired to smile.

Akello wanted to ask her father when her mother would get well, but she was afraid of the answer. There was no doctor in the village and the hospital was fifteen kilometres away. Her father reminded her that there was breakfast to cook. All her mother's work was Akello's now. Like her two older brothers and two younger sisters, Akello was in her uniform but there would be no school today.

It was no time for dancing and no time for dreams.

Now the baby was crying again.

"Let me," said Akello.

She lifted the small, warm boy with the creased forehead and tiny, dry fists. Akello held him carefully, and showered him with words soft enough to stroke him into sleep. He weighed little more than the chickens.

"Mother," said Akello, her eyes on the baby's fingers, no fatter than grains of corn, "what will you name him?"

But her mother did not answer. For a moment Akello thought she had given all her breath to the baby, and kept none for herself. But then her mother stretched out her fingers towards Akello, and nodded slightly.

"Madongo," she said, and turned over to sleep.

With porridge to cook, in the lean-to kitchen at the back of the house, Akello had to find a place to lie Madongo down on a blanket. After each stir of the heavy black pan she turned to smile at him and soothed him with her voice.

The morning was misty. Looking out from the village, Akello could not see the forest. She couldn't see the maize fields or matoke banana groves, or hear the horns of the boda-boda motorcycle taxis. Neither could she make out the muddy path that led to her school, or further on, to the creek where water must be fetched. Akello could hardly see her own little garden, where beans, cassava and sweet potatoes grew in the earth below, and fruit was ripening on the trees.

Somewhere in the forest called The Place of Darkness was the gorilla who had danced with her. Akello didn't know when she would see him again…

In the forest, Sanyu left the rest behind. He knew where people lived, with smoke and wheels and rhythms. He would find her.

Sanyu had not travelled far when he found a melon open on the ground, sliced in half, gleaming wet with sweetness. There was a dead bug stuck to it, so he flicked it off and ate that first. Then he sucked out the flesh of the fruit until the skin was thin and empty.

Sanyu felt sleepy now. When he stood he was unsteady. Sanyu began to knuckle-walk away, but he hardly knew where he was going. He found himself stumbling and lurching as the forest closed up in front of his heavy eyes.

When he heard the faint, blurred sound of broken twigs and leaves set aside, he thought the

girl was coming back for him, but he was too sleepy to look. And perhaps it was just a dream. His eyes were sealing and his feet were too heavy to lift from the ground.

He didn't know the net was there, even when it draped around him. He didn't feel the tug as it tightened like the blackness around him.

The last words of the day fell slowly and heavily, and in the classroom everyone felt their weight.

"No," Anya murmured.

Looking around her, she could see the shock on other faces.

Mr Eden's eyes were not laughing or bright and his face lay flat. He breathed a louder, longer breath than usual. Then he tried to bounce back into the real world but Anya could see that he hadn't really left the story behind.

Ryan started to hurry her up because they were going home together, but for Anyu it was hard to think about reading folders and P.E. kit when Sanyu was in danger and Akello was afraid.

She hoped it was the kind of story where things would be all right in the end. But even while they played at Ryan's house, she pictured Sanyu in the net, and Akello's mother too tired to wake.

4

When the children walked into the classroom Mr Eden said he'd flipped the day upside down.

"Story first?" asked Anya, feeling her eyes grow.

"And foremost," said Mr Eden, putting a box of tissues close enough for her to reach. "Is that all right?"

Anya just nodded and everyone else seemed to agree.

The baby was sleeping again. Akello wrapped the blanket around his chin and tiptoed back to the porridge. She hoped her mother would have the strength to eat a little, but she didn't want to wake her. She hoped Madongo would sleep long enough for her to go out for oil and sugar, tea and flour.

Once the pan had been emptied, and she'd scrubbed it clean and swept the floor, Akello left her sisters to watch the baby. The mist was lifting and the sun was brighter now. She waved to her father, digging sweet potatoes from the earth in the garden. Past the chickens she hurried, reminding herself to check for eggs when she returned.

Walking barefoot as always, Akello tried to hear music in her head but there was too much noise from the motorcycle engines and the horns. Traders shouted from the market stalls. She could smell the roasted meat. There was fish too. Some of it was slippery but the dried kind looked as tough as the soles of shoes.

There was no time to look at the second-hand clothes, or the rolls of bright cloth. Akello picked up a few candles, but did not buy, in case the coins in her pocket ran out.

Outside the mosque people gathered under a tent to respect the dead. Akello saw one of her classmates drinking soda. His grandma had died and the condolences would last forty days. The boy didn't see her. He was listening to a story. Akello wondered whether it was a true one, or the kind that was more like a dream, but could be true, or should be.

Sorry to be passing the school, Akello ran a few yards to the store where she could buy the sugar and tea. While she waited to be served because the shopkeeper was talking on his mobile phone, she heard the sound of a vehicle approaching. Akello saw a jeep lurching to a stop outside the store selling paraffin. Out of it stepped a group of white people in plain clothes.

There was a man with a backpack over his shoulder and a cigarette clenched between his lips for a moment before he drew in the smoke. Behind him was a woman, with straight hair hanging down like damp tails under a hat. The other man held a camera that he swung around, positioning the street in his lens.

Akello turned her head to one side. They were talking loudly but she couldn't understand what they said. The way they looked around them, with their eyes hidden by sunglasses, made Akello think they were surprised but not pleased.

A fat man was last to climb down from the jeep. His strange words sounded like a joke to Akello, but she couldn't see what was funny.

She supposed the white people were tourists. Her father had told Akello that from time to time they arrived in the village with money to spend.

They would be surrounded by children, who came away with sweets. Akello had never seen foreigners before. But she couldn't be sure about the black driver still sitting at the wheel, smoking but watching. Was he local? He looked strong enough to cut down trees and lift them up again. Did he speak her language?

The driver took no notice of Akello.

The woman waved and smiled, but kept on chewing. Akello knew her brothers and sisters would be glad of gum. When the woman beckoned her with one curly forefinger and a nod, she hesitated. Then she crossed the street and waited, smiling curiously. The woman's lips were glossy but frayed, and her cheeks looked as if they'd been scoured with stones. She'd burned. There was a rim of red skin around her neck that Akello thought must feel fiery.

"Hi," said the woman, and held out the pack of gum.

Akello slipped out one strip in its wrapper and smiled her thanks. The woman held the packet closer, as if she meant her to take more, so Akello pulled out strips for her brothers and sisters, which didn't leave many behind. The woman laughed.

"You like gum!"

Akello didn't understand for sure, but she guessed the meaning. She frowned because she wasn't greedy.

"Aw, you take it all, honey," said the woman, and handed her the pack, but Akello shook her head and hurried away.

"Hey, come back, honey!" cried the woman.

Akello didn't speak much English but she understood. She just didn't stop. Behind her she heard the fat man say something that amused him. He laughed in a way she didn't like but she tried to feel tall as she walked away.

Later, when Akello was on the way home with her shopping, she saw the jeep again. Under a tarpaulin at the back, something large and stiff was hidden but Akello could not guess what it might be. She thought the jeep was empty, but then she

saw the black man asleep in the driver's seat with his hat tipped forward to shade his face.

She glanced into the café and saw the rest of the group sitting behind tall, golden beers. She could tell from the lift of their voices that they were asking questions, sometimes overlapping. What did they want? There were no smart hotels. Nowhere to buy shampoo or perfume, lipstick or cream to soothe burnt skin.

It was none of her business and besides, the owner of the café seemed more than happy to be their host. Along with the beers, he had brought them his child, and the woman let him pull off her hat. Walking on, Akello heard the beat of a drum, and the visitors clapping.

Something made Akello hurry now. As she approached the house, the sound of Madongo's cries swelled through the chatter of the chickens. Akello rushed inside. Her sister held the baby, jiggling him over her shoulder and patting his back, but he did not stop wailing. Akello took him, and let him suck her finger. For a moment he was soothed but it was milk he wanted and soon his mouth was wide open again.

Her mother stirred, and reached for Madongo as if in her sleep. Soon he was suckling, and before long he too was asleep, his mouth parted and wet with milk.

"Will he take all her strength?" Akello asked, but her father was too anxious to answer.

For a few hours all was quiet inside. The boys were sent for water from the creek, taking plastic bottles to fill. Akello's sisters played without toys, chasing and hiding until Akello reminded them how to make letters, marking out their shapes with sticks in the ground. Remembering the gum, she gave them a strip each, and told them about the white people with their sunglasses and cameras.

Hearing Madongo crying once more, Akello returned to her mother's bedside. Her father's head had dropped forward, supported by both hands. He looked up slowly, and Akello saw his fear.

"She's sick," he said, and they looked to Akello's mother, her breathing tight, her forehead damp.

Akello remembered the jeep parked in the town with the man asleep under his hat. She told her father: white men, a black driver, a woman with gum. Big, fat wheels and a noisy engine.

"They can take us to the hospital," she told her father, "if we explain."

She was not sure how, but she would try.

Ryan knew what that meant. When heroes tried they always succeeded. Mr Eden's fists were tight but not angry. He looked as if he planned to run to the hospital himself. The children knew how much Mr Eden liked the word *determination*.

Anya's mum had been ill when she was very small and the treatment had made her hair fall out, but she was better now and Anya tried to forget how frightened she'd been. Now she remembered. Sometimes people did die, and in stories it didn't hurt so much because then you could try to close the book and keep them inside it. And they didn't really die at all because if you opened the book up, there they were.

"Mr Eden," she said, quietly, last one out of the door.

"Yes, Anya?" He smiled gently. "Don't worry. Love always wins. Love makes you brave and strong."

Anya smiled back.

5

At three o'clock Mr Eden called the children back to the carpet.

"Have you flipped the day back again?" asked Ryan.

"Yes," said Mr Eden. "It's a symmetrical day. It began with Story Time and that's how it's going to end."

Anya thought every day should be symmetrical but she took a tissue from the box and hid it up her sleeve.

As Akello ran back past the mosque she saw the jeep ahead of her, and heard its engine splutter awake. The driver was upright now, and impatient. Was she too late?

Now the jeep had gathered sound and speed. It hurtled towards her, as fast as the road allowed with its dips and bumps, its cracks and fall-away edges. Akello waved, but only the woman seemed to see her, and her quick wave had no smile to match. The jeep drew so close it would pass her by any second and be gone.

There was nothing else Akello could do.

She stepped out right in front of it.

There were shouts and a scream. A screech and a swerve. The driver jerked the wheel round. Akello didn't stop. She was afraid the vehicle would turn again and leave her behind – like a dead bird, or an old exhaust that had broken away and become an obstacle.

Instead she stepped in front again. Akello shouted, knowing they would not understand the words but hoping they would recognise their meaning.

"Stop! Help me please!"

The engine fell silent but the people did not. They were all talking at once, at her. Akello heard anger, but it was in the language she barely spoke. The driver narrowed his eyes at her, as if she stood in the sun. In her own language, sharply, accusingly, he asked what she thought she was doing.

Relieved, Akello told him her mother was sick and the baby was hungry.

"Please, sir, will you drive them to the hospital?"

She told him where it was and how far but he cut her short as if he knew. There was an argument. Akello needed no English to understand that some of them wanted to drive on – all but the woman, who reached out and beckoned. Akello wasn't sure, but she sensed that the woman had won. She climbed into the jeep beside her, but there were no smiles as the engine started up again.

The driver shouted back, asking for directions to her house. In a minute they were there, and Akello's father led her mother towards the jeep – slowly, too slowly for the passengers. Akello's sister brought Madongo wrapped in a shirt and crying. She gave him to Akello.

"They're not infectious?" asked the driver.

Akello shook her head, hoping. Her father was talking, agitated. He wanted to come but there was no room.

"What about the back?" he asked.

He pointed to the trailer with its bumped-up tarpaulin, but the driver pushed out a hand that meant *No.*

"Stay with your children," he told Akello's father.

He revved up the engine and soon they left the house behind. In moments the village was behind them too. Akello was frightened by the speed and the jolts, the wrenching turns and the voices clashing. They were moving so fast that Akello felt sure they would reach the hospital in no time. It could not be soon enough.

From behind there were noises: the tarpaulin twitching in wind, or something heavy sliding or turning underneath it. At first the white people paid no attention, but as the sounds became more regular Akello saw the driver look hard into the mirror. The woman seemed to want him to drive faster.

Trees leaned close to the road, and knocked the jeep from time to time with a low branch or wide, flapping leaves. The wind grew stronger and louder. It gusted under the wheels and dragged the woman's hair around her face. The fidgeting map on the fat man's lap tried to lift folded wings to fly.

Madongo was fractious. Even though Akello tried to hold him safe against her chest, his grizzling stopped only for him to find the strength to start again. The sound of his hunger broke weakly through the bumping, the engine's growl and whine, the thuds and flurries.

Akello tried to bat away the cigarette smoke that blew in his face. She was glad her mother slept.

The driver told the others something in English, something unwelcome. Whatever he wanted or decided, they were protesting, but in the mirror she saw his face set firm. He brought the jeep to a halt, and left it leaning a little, so that it tilted off the broken edge of the track and nosed down into the forest. Walking away into the undergrowth, he stopped, and stood still with his legs apart. Before the woman covered Akello's eyes she knew that the beer had worked its way through and he needed to relieve himself.

The three other men reconsidered. Soon they were all finishing their cigarettes and dropping them to empty their own bladders. Akello was left in the jeep with the woman scowling, her mother stirring and Madongo crying. She backed away from the woman's lightly greased hand and a wrist that smelt of flowers. But when she turned her head towards the noises behind, she saw something strange. The tarpaulin seemed to be moving of its own accord.

The woman pulled her round again by the shoulders. Madongo began to wail and squirm. His body bent in the middle as if his stomach gave him pain.

The woman shouted at the men, but they were coming anyway, running towards the jeep. Akello saw that their eyes, still hidden by sunglasses, were fixed on the tarpaulin. It began to thrash like a giant fish out of water. Something live was underneath it, something living but sick – or dying?

The noise that tore out from the tarpaulin was a grunt Akello knew.

In the back of the jeep Sanyu's strength was stirring through each limb. His world was black and closed around him, but he stretched his chest against the net that wrapped him. He gripped the tough thread between his fists and tugged. He opened up his legs and kicked his feet as if the mesh might burst like a melon. Through the thick, oily roof that bent stiffly into folds above the net, he could smell people. Smoke. Sweat. Thinly he heard voices through his own clatter and floundering. Sanyu needed sweeter air. He needed the green light he trusted.

He felt other limbs and smaller hands reaching for him in the darkness, but Sanyu's were stronger. With all his force he ripped open the soft cage that clung to him and knocked away the tarpaulin, drawing himself onto his feet. The men leapt back. Sanyu heard a cry he recognised. The girl in the dress was there, trapped like he had been, and he must free her.

As he opened his mouth to scare the men away, the wind carried a different smell that gathered in his throat and nostrils. Not human smoke but thicker, wilder, it lit the green with flame.

Smelling it too, Akello saw the fire start to dance. When she stepped down from the seat with Madongo in her arms, the woman made no move to stop her. She was too busy yelling at the driver, who searched a bag on the floor of the jeep, swearing, looking up and swearing again. At the sight of the gorilla rising loud and angry above the other men, he placed one hand back on the wheel.

The shouts were sharp and sudden with panic. Like the smoke, the men whirled. The fat one ran towards the jeep but the wind blew the flames at his heels. Taller than Madongo, the fire hissed and cracked. It was a flickery, waving wall that surged and lifted, fast and fattening, towards the trees.

Firelight warmed Madongo's face. Akello looked back to the jeep, its front wheels fringed with fire. Still her mother slept but the men were bundling back into the seats and shouting to the driver.

"Mother, wake up!" cried Akello.

The engine choked into life. Sanyu charged towards the jeep. The people cowered as he lifted Akello's mother in his strong, black arms. Roaring, the jeep staggered and began to jolt away.

Sanyu did not care about the vehicle turning its back on the forest and the fire, and shrinking down the road. He knew he must stretch higher than the flames. He saw the woman crumpling unsteadily to her feet. Caught by the wind, the edge of her dress teased the fire that swelled close. Sanyu picked her up and ran with her, placed her down ahead of the fire, and ran back again.

The baby cried face-down on Akello's shoulder. Ripping a trail of cord from the net that had caged him, Sanyu helped her criss-cross it so that it made a pouch. Madongo's legs and arms hung free but he was fastened to Akello. She nodded, thankfully. Now her arms were free to help her gather the speed she needed.

Then Sanyu ran back for her mother. He lifted the woman around his shoulders, wearing her like a scarf. But he pulled the cloth tightly around her thighs so that it did not trickle and tempt the flame. To Sanyu she felt bird-like, with bones thin enough to snap. His grip must be gentle but firm.

Akello pointed north, towards the village where the doctor worked. Sanyu understood.

"Follow me," he told Akello, with his grunt and his eyes.

With the woman across his shoulders he must take care. But he must knuckle-walk faster than flame. Akello was his partner and she must match him. They must leap. Together they must dance as never before.

Chased by wind, the fire was fast. The air thickened with heat and angry light. Smoke began to tickle his nostrils and throat. Sanyu could no longer smell the river but he knew that not far away it would be running, cool and quick. He knew that water made a softer wall, one that could protect them. His senses had been deadened by the tranquiliser. Now they were overwhelmed. Yet somehow he knew where to find the river.

Quickly they made their way deeper into the forest, with the fire tracking them like a hunter. When they felt it gaining on them they surged forward in the widest, highest jumps they could make. As Akello followed the gorilla, the sounds of Madongo's whimpers blurred with the snap and crack of wood turning black, of smoke thickening and flames growling like a predator. The wind beat the world around her and the fire ate it up. But Akello was strong. She could outrun the fire. It only jerked and twisted and sneaked and snatched. Let it crackle around her ankles! Akello could dance.

Sanyu knew the river was close now. Through the sounds there was one that rippled on, flowing and splashing over stones. He reached out a hand to Akello, because she was just a girl and her heart must be tiring. Her grip felt firm. Together they wove their way towards the water, until Sanyu's ears rang with its song.

And there it was, shining ahead, fast and cool and full of softer light. They must follow it to its widest swell, where it rounded like a pool and deepened down. Now they reached it – the crossing point. Sanyu stopped. He looked at Akello. She was breathing hard. Heat beaded her forehead with sweat. The distance across the water was too far for the wind to drag the fire. But was it too far for an exhausted girl to leap?

Sanyu hurled himself towards the river. On the edge of its bank, he lifted off like a great hairy bird,

his legs astride and high, opening wide in the air and gliding on. Over the flowing water he leapt, landing beyond the reeds.

Looking back at Akello, he saw the fire rising behind her, taller every moment, closer.

As the army of flames advanced, she lifted her chest and ran. Then she jumped, arms outstretched – as if it was the trees she meant to clear and the sky she hoped to reach. The brightness below was flecked and dazzling as she crossed it. One foot splashed at the river's edge but the other landed on grass. The fire hissed but it could not follow.

The girl and the gorilla breathed a long, deep breath. The air was sweeter and cleaner now.

Akello knew the hospital could not be far away.

"We're safe, Madongo," she murmured. "It's all right now."

The story had spilt out faster than usual, racing and sometimes almost tumbling. Mr Eden looked exhausted and hot. He fanned his head with his hand.

"Is that the end?" asked someone.

"No," said Anya and others shook their heads.

"Stories have a climax," said Mr Eden, "but they also need an ending. That'll be tomorrow."

Ryan told Javeen in the corridor that he hoped there would be no kissing. Anya didn't want the last words to be *happily ever after* because that was harder to believe in than gorillas dancing.

Anya didn't make up her own ending but she dreamed one, and when she woke it was lost.

6

The children knew this was the day the story ended. All through English and Maths, Science and Topic they waited. Mr Eden looked very thoughtful as they gathered around him at 2:58.

It was two days since the doctor had taken in three new patients, one of them handed over by a young male gorilla. He'd become used to the blackback who slept outside, kept watch and never strayed far from the hospital.

The girl in school uniform had arrived smudged by smoke and ash. Her breathing was tight and she had no strength left in her legs. Now she was his helper. The doctor called her Nurse Akello and he would have liked six more like her.

Most days his only assistant was a backpacking student who had stopped by because the doctor knew his father, but stayed to volunteer. The boy, who was only eighteen, had needed a good haircut first. Dr Odoki thought he'd be better suited to a circus, but he made Akello laugh.

Baby Madongo was doing well. The doctor was glad for the family. He could see how relieved the student was – a soft boy who'd already seen a child die. Soon Madongo's mother would have her own milk to give him. She had needed antibiotics but she was walking now, and Dr Odoki hoped that in the morning she could leave.

Dusk was falling. The rain that had put out the fire had also cooled the air. The doctor saw the mother close her eyes as she looked down on her sleeping baby.

"You can clock off," he told Akello quietly. "End of shift."

She smiled, and looked outside. The doctor and the student exchanged glances. They knew she was looking for the gorilla.

"Take a walk," said Dr Odoki. "But don't go far."

The young student was sweeping the floor.

"You've done enough, James," the doctor told him in English, "for one day."

Akello had gone by the time the student had washed his hands. While the doctor checked the supply of bandages, syringes and medication, the young man said goodnight to each patient, asleep or awake.

The student looked into the fading light but Akello had disappeared. In the compound outside, a cat sat on the roof of Dr Odoki's truck. A bird

perched on the top of a crate, but nothing moved. Quietness had shrouded everything as the light ebbed away. The ground was still damp, and here and there puddles glinted. The moon was full.

The student was hungry but something kept him there, looking out towards the forest. Hoping. As the darkness thickened around the hospital, he heard something which took him to the doorway. Not the cat, or a bird, not an engine or a voice. But something was outside, alive and moving. The student peered through the twilight, sure that the young gorilla was out there somewhere. He was about to call out into the bushes for Akello to come in when he saw that she was there.

For a moment the moonlight found her face. And for a moment the young student thought she was flying.

As his eyes adjusted to the light he followed the line of her arms, now straight, now curved. He saw that she was spinning. Leaping. Balancing on one leg, or ten toes. She didn't dance alone.

His coat as dark as the evening light, the gorilla held her high. He raised her like a fallen star. He trailed her like a gown that whirled around his legs. From his arms she hung like a ladder, swung like rope and fluttered like a moth. In his arms she speared and rolled, and laced the twilight. Silvered and gleaming, the pair of them streamed. Curling and overlapping, they sparked like fireflies. They etched the darkness with patterns more intricate than cobwebs and bolder than sunset. So light were their steps that the evening hush gathered unbroken around them.

As the student watched, the dancers held him like a spell.

In London the young man had seen Swan Lake, Coppelia and Giselle. He had applauded some of the world's greatest dancers. But he had never seen a *pas de deux* so joyful or so strange, with such a wild and mysterious beauty.

At its end he had no flowers to throw at the ballerina's feet. He raised his hands to clap, but the silence felt so delicate he did not want to tear it. Instead he held his arms high.

By the light of the moon he saw Akello's eyes meet his as the gorilla lowered her gently to the ground. He saw their happiness.

"Thank you," he whispered.

Akello curtseyed. Sanyu bowed.

The student nodded, and smiled. Turning back

to the beds where the patients slept, he wondered whether anyone in Uganda, in Africa or the world beyond, would dream that night of anything so unreal, so soft and thick with magic. It was too secret to share but too beautiful to forget.

As he checked each bed in turn, the student allowed himself a beginner's shimmy, and a sudden, stumbling pirouette.

Mr Eden shimmied and pirouetted too. He didn't stumble, and everyone clapped. Mr Eden bowed.

Ryan was mouthing, *"James!"* because he knew what the J stood for after the MR and before the EDEN on the classroom door.

Some of the others hadn't noticed the name the doctor called the student but Anya was sure his hair was floppy and fair. She gave Mr Eden a small smile. Inside her there was a bigger smile, hiding, but that was for Sanyu and Akello.

"Did they ever dance again?" she asked.

"What do you think?" asked Mr Eden.

"Yes," said Anya, almost in a whisper, because she felt sure that the dances would always be secrets.

Mr Eden winked. The classroom was quiet. No one moved until Mr Eden reminded them it was time to go home.

Ryan lifted his chest. In his deepest voice he growled, "Me, Mukasa!"

Anya wondered whether the real silverback ever knew the truth about Sanyu.

Collecting her things from her drawer, she let the others leave first. In the doorway she looked back at the space the story had filled, but it was just a carpet now. The story was inside her.

Mr Eden looked up from his desk.

"Did you like Sanyu's story?" he called.

Anya nodded. Then, in the doorway, she remembered the student in the Ugandan hospital.

She raised her hands in the air.

Two hours later Mr Eden opened his front door to a sound that wasn't quite a word.

"DA!"

His wife appeared in the hall and they embraced.

"Good day?" he asked and she nodded and smiled.

"Me too," he told her. "Lucky man."

Mr Eden grinned. He smiled at the carved gorilla looking down on him from the windowsill in the hall, where it liked to hoot at the postwoman every morning.

"DA!" came through the kitchen doorway, louder and higher than before and wobbly with bounce.

"Da – da!" cried Mr Eden, as he burst into the kitchen like a performer springing onto a stage, arms wide.

He saw a couple of bananas in the fruit bowl and tried to stick the stem ends in his ears.

Their son laughed wildly. He was wriggling with excitement, but fixed to the high chair with a plastic bib round his neck. Mushy food that Mr Eden couldn't quite identify had collected in its pocket. More was stuck to his cheeks and chin. The little boy was only eleven months old but he knew the sound of his father's key in the lock. He knew how to grab, too – and as Mr Eden leaned down to

kiss the small (lightly splattered) forehead, he grabbed one banana and hit the top of his daddy's head.

The other fell to the floor, and as its skin split, Mr Eden peeled open the rest and took the largest bite he could manage. His son laughed and pointed at his naughty daddy.

"Our supper's almost ready," said his wife, "if you're not too full already."

She wiped their son clean, removed the bib and and lifted him out of the high chair. Now he could cling to his father – rather like a trace of yesterday's food clung to the kitchen wall. The stain was just below the photo of the Ugandan hospital where his parents had first met, long ago and far away, before they met again online.

Akello Eden saw her husband remembering. She kissed his cheek.

"Story time," said Mr Eden, taking the little boy and twitching his nose when a sticky hand squeezed it.

Suddenly he waltzed his son into the hall and turned a sharp tango head at the foot of the stairs.

"Don't make him throw up, darling!" called Akello Eden.

Carefully James Eden carried his laughing passenger into the lounge and sat down with his legs wide. That way the baby could fit his nappy-fat bottom into the gap and lean his back against his father's stomach. David Sanyu Eden was reaching and grunting. His father lifted up the soft toy gorilla with the red bow in her hair and sat her facing Sanyu where she could listen too. He made a mental note that Gladys, who felt rather dribbly, would need a spin in the washing machine while David slept. Mr Eden gave her a spin, lifting one furry leg and helping her to balance on the other. David Sanyu Eden knocked her over.

"Aaaagh!" cried Mr Eden, falling back on the carpet so that his son could tickle him and roll over his chest.

"That doesn't sound much like a story," said Akello, watching them with a smile.

"You got me!" cried her husband. "Where's my story gone?" he searched under Gladys and the yellow plastic truck. "David Sanyu Eden! Have you taken my story? Have you eaten it?"

His son laughed, and looked underneath the potty that he hadn't quite learned to use. Mr Eden laughed even louder.

David's parents agreed that he wasn't really tired enough for bed. So they ate their supper on their laps to keep him company as he crawled and chattered wordlessly around the playpen, stopping now and then to stick his head between the plastic bars and growl happily.

While he played, Mr Eden heard about Akello's day. Then later, when the plates were empty and David became warm and still on his lap, he took him upstairs to bed, not with waltzes or tangos but whispers and strokes.

In the smallest bedroom he settled his son in the cot, under the duvet with Gladys. Akello pulled the curtains to blot out the lights from the street. Car tyres swished below but on the glass the rain was lighter than birdsong.

David was very sleepy but he willed his eyelids upwards and managed a "Da" that wasn't much louder than a breath. This time it meant *story*.

"This one won't make him wild," Mr Eden promised his wife, in his softest voice.

She smiled, turned off the light and sat on the carpet to hear it too. James Eden remembered. He gave a kiss to each member of his audience (apart from Gladys, who was slobbery enough already) and began.

"In a school not too far away from here there was a teacher who spent all day surrounded by children. Some of them didn't always know whether they were wild or tame, but they had magic power. They were dancing gorillas, every one of them – even the ones who didn't know a single step, and found gorilla ballet hard to believe in."

David Sanyu Eden was asleep now. Mr Eden lowered his voice, and smiled at Akello.

"And the teacher was glad of their magic," he whispered, "because it set him free."

About Sue Hampton

Sue Hampton has twenty books across different genres for children and teenagers, including TRACES (top three in The People's Book Prize 2012) and FRANK (bronze in The Wishing Shelf Award 2103). Her writing has been praised by her hero Michael Morpurgo ("terrific" "enthralling" "beautifully written"). An ex-teacher based in Herts, Sue now visits schools to inspire pupils. She is also an ambassador for Alopecia UK and has seen that stories can change lives. In her work you can always find love, courage and the right to be different.

Connect with Sue Hampton

For details of her other work, for adults, teenagers and children, see www.suehamptonauthor.co.uk

About Mary Casserley

Artist Mary Casserley works in the art department at Berkhamsted School and has produced two books, Berkhamsted High Street and Postcards from Berkhamsted. She loves to draw buildings and enjoyed creating gorillas for a change!
http://www.1sthouseportraits.com/

Book(s) by Sue Hampton
Pomp and Circumstances, ISBN 9781782281818
On Royal Wedding Day James isn't in the mood for romance after a disastrous date. His little sister's off to Hyde Park, and somewhere in the crowd he won't be joining is a girl from a different kind of postcode who could change his world. For five young Londoners, one day will bring panic, grief and conflict, and risks worth taking.

Aliens and Angels: Three Stories For Christmas, ISBN 9781782283157
Sue Hampton captures the spirit of Christmas with three warm-hearted stories full of humour, mystery and magic – starring a boy who'd rather be an angel than a globalob, a donkey called Trouble and a girl with a cracker-sized lamb. With illustrations by children from schools Sue has visited, this is a book to make you smile at any time of year.

Lightning Source UK Ltd.
Milton Keynes UK
UKOW03f0642260914

239162UK00001BA/9/P